# TREASURE
## of
# Watchdog Mountain
## The Story of a Mountain in the Catskills

# Alf Evers

**Newly Illustrated Edition**
**Art by Christie Scheele**

This Woodstocker Books/Arthur Schwartz & Co. revised edition of *The Treasure of Watchdog Mountain* has been produced with the approval of the estate of Alf Evers.

Woodstocker Books/Arthur Schwartz & Co.
15 Meads Mountain Road
Woodstock, NY, 12498
www.woodstockerbooks.com
Orders: 800-669-9080

ISBN-13: 978-1-879504-19-6
ISBN-10: 1-879-504-19-7

Book design by Naomi Schmidt, Naomi Graphics
Art by Christie Scheele
Back cover photograph by Andrea Barrist Stern
Map reprinted with permission of NYS Department of Environmental Conservation

Produced in the United States of America
Printed by CraftPrint, Singapore

# Acknowledgments

The following assisted our efforts in bringing this book to print: Ed Sanders, who introduced us to Alf. Bill Rudge, of the Department of Environmental Conservation in New Paltz, offered expertise and enthusiasm. Teacher Jeff Fingerman provided vital suggestions. We thank also proofreader Steve Hoare for his professionalism and Debbie Allen of Black Dome Press for her help. Helen Budrock, assistant director, and Aaron Bennett, director of education, the Catskill Center for Conservation and Development, gave support and, in particular, guidance in updating the material in the latter part of the book.

Revisions and changes were made in consultation with Alf's son, Kit Evers, whose editorial suggestions and knowledge of mountain life proved invaluable. We are grateful for the assistance of geologist Robert Titus. Woodstocker Books, associate Deborah Day, as always, offered subtle and useful suggestions on key points. Joanne Sackett, the children's librarian at the Woodstock Library, has been a friend of this project from the start. We also thank Mary McNamara, John Bierhorst, Tom O'Brien, Joshua Kaufman and the Corning Museum of Glass library for their assistance.

Designer Naomi Schmidt and artist Christie Scheele not only provided their talents but helped us to create a synergistic team – and we wish to acknowledge their enormous contribution.

*Jo and Arthur Schwartz*

Some of my illustrations were inspired by works of art already in existence, so I would like to tip my hat to Van Gogh, Sorolla, and several oil paintings of my own that are out in the world leading their own lives.

*Christie Scheele*

Funding for this book was provided, in part, through a contribution in memory of Alf Evers from:
The Catskill Center for Conservation and Development
PO Box 504, Route 28, Arkville, NY 12406, (845) 586-2611, www.catskillcenter.org
The Catskill Center is a regionally-based, non-profit membership organization working to protect the cultural, historic, and natural resources of the Catskill Mountains.

*To find out about environmental issues in the Catskill Mountain region, contact any of these organizations.*

**Catskill Center for Conservation and Development**,
P.O. Box 504, Route 28, Arkville, New York 12406 • (845) 568-2611
www.catskillcenter.org • cccd@catskillcenter.org

**New York State Department of Environmental Conservation**, **Region 3**,
21 South Putt Corner Road, New Paltz, New York 12561 • (845) 256-3092
www.dec.state.ny.us • wprudge@gw.dec.state.ny.us

**Woodstock Land Conservancy**,
P.O. Box 864, Woodstock, New York 12498 • (845) 334-2418
www.woodstocklandconservancy.org • info@woodstocklandconservancy.org

**Open Space Institute,**
1350 Broadway, suite 201, New York, New York 10018-7799 • (212) 290-8200
www.osiny.org • info@osiny.org

**The Nature Conservancy,**
PO Box 453, 43355 State Highway 28, Arkville, New York • (845) 586-1002
www.nature.org • awhite@tnc.org

# About Alf Evers

Alf Evers was probably the only ninety-nine-year-old author ever to have finished a 500-page book. He died on December 29, 2004. This was thirty-three days before his 100th birthday. His last book, *Kingston: City on the Hudson*, was published in 2005. He worked on it for twelve years, and wrote every day. Meanwhile, he had also started on his next book, about one of Woodstock's art colonies.

The only way Alf could see to correct his manuscript was with two magnifying glasses held together with a rubber band. This was much better than the magnifiers you purchased at the store, he said, and he had always liked "inventing things." He was blind in one eye and could barely see out of the other. But he examined thousands of pages of his manuscript. His friend and helper, Ed Sanders, had typed it in very large type and double-spaced it so he could read it.

Alf loved the land and climbed mountains in the Catskills when he was in his nineties. But he was born in the Bronx in 1905 in a time when there were still horse and buggies, and streets were lit by gaslight. His father was a painter and architect. Just before World War I, the family moved to a farm in Tillson. Later, his parents gave up farming and bought the Hasbrouck House on Huguenot Street in New Paltz. Alf helped his father restore the famous stone house.

He and his older sister attended New Paltz High School. Several teachers got him interested in local history when they took him to old gravestones and showed him Native American artifacts.

He went to Hamilton College and then to the Arts Students League in New York City to study painting and drawing. By the time he graduated, it was the Depression and work was scarce. One of his occupations was as an investigator for an insurance company. He said this work taught him to be a good researcher.

He started writing children's books with his wife, an illustrator. They produced over fifty children's books, including *The Deer Jackers* and *The House the Pecks Built*.

His varied careers also included farmer, landscape gardener, writer of greeting card verses, and artist. Many people have collected his drawings and paintings.

Alf's favorite subject involved the people, the legends, animals, flowers, trees and mountains of the Catskill region. His adult books included: *The Catskills: From Wilderness to Woodstock; Woodstock, History of an American Town*; and *In Catskill Country: Collected Essays on Mountain History, Life and Lore*. He contributed articles to newspapers and magazines. He served as an officer of the New York State Folklore Society and on the board of the Catskill Center for Conservation and Development; he was president of the Woodstock Library. He was honorary chairman of the Save Overlook Committee of the Woodstock Land  Conservancy and also Woodstock's town historian. In 2001, he was honored for his contributions in furthering New York State history.

Alf said that if you want to understand a town, you need to learn to understand all the other towns around it. And, you read books on them. Then you read about the state and the country and the planet. Then your thoughts take you to outer space. He said that maybe some day there will be space travelers who will bring back local histories to people on our planet. He found being an historian the most exciting work possible.

To the very end of his life, you could always get Alf's help on a project. He was courteous and kind.

# Table of Contents

*"When we try to pick out anything by itself, we find it hitched to everything else in the universe."*
John Muir

# 1
# THE MOUNTAIN

Old Mr. Wills, who lives on Artist's Rock Farm in the valley beneath Watchdog Mountain, likes to point out to visitors how much like a dog the mountain looks when seen from the top of the big rock near his apple orchard.

"See that long sweep over there – well that's the dog's back," says Mr. Wills. "Now over that way, where you see the cliff sorta tumbling down – that's his face. And those ridges to the north, they sure look like he's stretching out. Yessir, that mountain looks like an old dog a-guarding the valley. That's why the first settlers and the Indians who used to l i v e around here called it Watchdog Mountain."

Most of the time Mr. Wills and the other valley people simply call it "the Old Dog." On hot August afternoons when the low rumbling of thunder can be heard from far off behind the mountain, they say, "The Old Dog is growling – that means rain's a-coming." And when November mists swirl around the mountain's top the old people say, as their fathers said before them, "Looks like the Old Dog is smoking his pipe."

The valley people did not always have this friendly feeling toward their mountain, for they coveted treasures they thought to be hidden on it. They schemed and worked and fought to take them, leaving scars that still show clearly on the mountain's rocks and soil and even on its living things.

Today they try to be at peace with their mountain. After making many costly mistakes, they have come to understand what its real treasure is. They know that it cannot be greedily snatched away from the Watchdog. It must be used with an understanding of what it is, how it came into being and what its future is likely to be.

For this treasure is a part of that great treasure of plants and animals, of water, soil and minerals without which we could not live. And once destroyed, it may be gone forever, for it was built up slowly over billions of years.

## THE BEGINNING

No one is sure just how Watchdog Mountain was created. But it seems likely that the matter of which it was formed was once part of an ancient cloud of thin substance afloat in space from which our world emerged. This substance went through many changes until part of it became the hot liquid whirling ball which became our planet, the Earth. As the ball cooled, a rocky crust formed. Air and clouds with rain came into being. Soon great storms rained great oceans. The

2

# The Mountain

torrents wore away part of the crust turning it into sand lying at the bottom of a sea and along its shores. The earth lifted its sands into many land masses with high mountains. Then rains wore them down again. This happened over and over as the Earth grew old. The various land masses moved. As they collided with one other, our continents were created.

One of these collisions created the mountain ranges in today's New England – pushed up as part of a much larger mass. Watchdog Mountain was part of that mass. Wind and water, and later on, frost and ice, carved away most of the mass and turned it into mud. The mud became sediment. It hardened into the sandstones that made the rocky bones of Watchdog Mountain. Something like the shape of the mountain the valley people know today appeared at last.

Even before the sandstones of Watchdog were formed, there had been life on earth. Unable, like all living things, to remain at rest, tiny flecks that first came into being in the sea, changed. Some left fossils, prints of their bodies, that can still be seen in the mountain's rocks.

The early forms of life adapted themselves to the varying conditions of heat and light and moisture found on the Earth. And so there arose the great brotherhood of living things that now covers our lands and floats in our waters, drawing the strength to maintain itself from sun and soil and water and air.

As the mountain took shape, many living things gradually came together on its sides. They were not discouraged by changes in climate or by the sheets of ice that sometimes crept down from the north and swept the mountain almost clean of life and soil down to its very rocks.

At last, the mountain came to be almost covered with a dense forest which clung to its steep sides like a coat of shaggy fur. On moist shallow soil and along the many brooks, hemlocks made a perpetual twilight with their heavy branches. Oak and chestnut trees grew in sunnier, drier places; maples stood here and there among the hemlocks. Gnarled old beeches were grouped in companies on richer soil with their young trees huddled around them. On the upper part of the mountain, wind-battered spruce grew in the shallow soil caught in rock crevices. They grew so slowly they changed hardly at all in the length of a man's life.

The mountain's living coat was woven of many threads, some large and strong, others slender and delicate, and some invisible. Dwarfed by the mighty trees above them, mushrooms, pink lady slippers and green ferns pushed up through the thick carpet of

# The Mountain

fallen leaves and hemlock needles that covered the forest floor.

Mosses and lichens clung to trees and rocks. Grapevines flowered and fruited in treetops.

Within the soil itself little plants and animals led their lives. When their lifeless bodies returned to the Earth, they became food for new living things.

Millions and millions of insects hummed and buzzed and burrowed in sun and shade. Tiny spiders hung their webs from rocks and leaves.

Birds nested in the trees, squirrels picked up acorns on the ground, trout swam and beaver built dams in the brooks. In open places where old trees had been blown down by winter gales, big-eyed rabbits played in the tangles of blackberry and huckleberry bushes which had sprung up. There, deer tasted the buds of young trees and wildcats watched from behind the fallen trunks for unwary mice gathering berry seeds.

Each kind of living thing depended on others for its food, and each in turn supplied food for still others. The community was not altogether calm. Plants competed fiercely for sunlight and food. Animals competed for mates and for places in which to bring up their young. Small animals were kept alert and strong, because only those who did could escape the larger animals to whom their bodies furnished food. Flowers competed, with color and scent, for the visits of insects without whose help they could not produce seeds.

The nation of plants and animals changed as winter and summer, cold seasons or hot ones, rain or drought, encouraged some living things to increase and others to lessen. But the sides of the old mountain were always astir with vigorous life – with the whir of wings, the patter of seeds dropping to earth on frosty mornings, the silent movement of roots downward through the moist soil, and the steady beating of uncountable animal hearts.

## Treasure of Watchdog Mountain

A few thousand years ago – only yesterday in the life of a mountain – a new and different being arrived to become part of the community. This member was far wiser than any other ever to live there. He was capable of kindness and generosity. He could understand many things which did not even exist to the deer and bears and squirrels. But with all his miraculous gifts of soul and heart and mind, he was to bring great trouble to the mountain – for he was man.

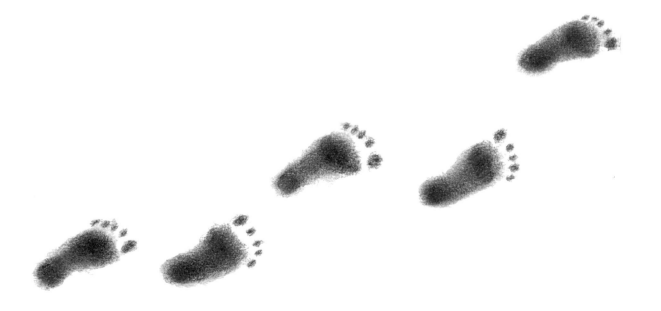

# 2
# Indian Treasure

The first men to see Watchdog Mountain and to find treasure there were Indian settlers. Gradually, these Indians worked out a way of living that was suited to the land on which they lived. They became part of the valley and mountain communities, and good neighbors of the old Watchdog. They never dreamed that their stay in the valley would end in violence, sadness and tragedy. But step by step they moved closer to this end. And without knowing it, they themselves were to help in bringing about their own downfall.

But for many years the people led quiet lives as hunters, farmers and craftsmen. They lived in bark-covered huts set on the knolls that bordered the rich plains along Watchdog Creek. The women, with the help of children and old men, planted fields of corn, beans, pumpkins and tobacco while the men hunted or fished. Their crops grew well, although their only farming tools were made from edged stones and shoulder bones of deer. For the soil was rich with fertility brought down from the mountain forests by many spring floods.

The people became skillful at making arrowheads, canoes, and fur and leather clothing. They were strong and handsome, for the soil from which they drew their strength was good.

In the fall the men left the old people and women to guard their villages while they went on hunting trips to the lower slopes of Watchdog. There they lived in shallow caves in the rocky ledges and hunted the deer and bears who had come there to fatten for the winter on the beechnuts, acorns and chestnuts strewn on the ground. They ate venison and bear meat until they, too, were fat. The women prepared the skins of the animals for clothing and dried some of the meat to eat with their corn and beans in the winter to come.

Sometimes it happened that late spring frosts killed the flower buds of the mountain nut trees. Then the Indians would find no fat deer and bears waiting for them in the fall. They would have to face a lean winter, even in their land of plenty.

The native people, in those days of peace with the old Watchdog, often looked up at the mountain with awe and happiness. For they believed that this mountain, which looked so much like a friendly, protecting dog, was the home of wise and wonder-working gods. These gods had hidden a great treasure on top of the mountain. It was a treasure of sunshine and rain, of stars and of the moon, all kept safe in a bark hut.

The Indians believed their gods opened the door of the hut to share some of the treasure. Every morning they let out the sun. And when night came they took in the sun and let out the moon and stars. Sometimes, they sent out wind and rain and snow, and when these had done their work the gods took them in again.

8

# Indian Treasure

They seldom climbed to the top of Watchdog Mountain. It would be wrong to disturb the mountain gods in their homes, for the gods might become angry. They might keep rain and sun, clouds and stars locked up. The rich valley might then become a gray desert in which nothing could live.

The years of peace with the mountain neared their end one fall afternoon, as the shadow of the mountain began to creep slowly across their valley. For days, strange stories had been coming to the Indians. Something as yet unknown to them had come from the sea and was gliding up their river. Perhaps this was a sea monster; perhaps it was a great water bird; perhaps it was something so new it did not even have a name. Silent groups of Indians watched and waited on the river bank.

What this mysterious thing coming toward them was, they could only guess. But they saw the work of their gods in everything and felt their presence everywhere. So this mysterious object must be something sent to them by their gods. Perhaps the gods themselves were coming to visit them.

Hours of patient waiting went by. Then an Indian motioned as a patch of white slipped out from behind the hill down the river. Slowly the patch moved toward them. It grew larger and began to take on a form. It was the sail of a ship from across the sea. But this the Indians could not know, for they had never seen or heard of such a thing before.

The ship glided closer. They glanced at each other and then at Watchdog Mountain. And seeing the mountain lying there friendly as always, the Indians felt courage to face whatever might come.

Quickly they slipped into their canoes. They paddled toward the ship. They listened intently to new sounds coming across the water – to the flapping of sails in the breeze, to the creaking of ropes, to the sound of sailors' voices and the rattling of shoes on the ship's deck.

As canoes and shipcame closer together, the men in canoes saw the men on the ship watching them from the deck and from perches in the rigging. They thought that whether these creatures were gods or not, they were strange and new. For their faces were pale and their cheeks were pink. Some had yellow hair and some wore beards. It was doubtful that these men were gods. For everyone knew that the gods had dark skin and hair and eyes. They looked much like themselves.

The newcomers smiled at the Indians and beckoned them with friendly gestures to come on board. They let ropes down the side of their ship to help the men climb to the deck. Some overcame their doubts and climbed nimbly up the ropes.

Europeans and Indians eyed each other shyly yet eagerly, wondering at each other's clothing and features and listening without understanding to each other's words. One of the men who had come on the ship, seeing a man wearing a beaver skin, asked by signs from where it came. The Indian pointed to the hazy blue shadow at the base of Watchdog Mountain. He explained with his hands that many beaver lived in the marshy land at the foot of the mountain and along the lower parts of its streams.

The eyes of the newcomers grew brighter as they stared at the mountain. They smiled and talked among themselves while stroking

# Indian Treasure

the soft fur worn by the Indian. One of the men held out a few brightly colored glass beads in the palm of his hands. He made signs to show that he would give these in exchange for the beaver skin.

The Indian smiled. He took the beads and gave up his fur. These beings may be gods after all, he thought, for only gods could be so generous. It was not hard to take beaver through the ice of their ponds in the winter. But beads like these were marvels such such as no one in the valley had ever seen.

The Europeans knew nothing of the treasure of wind and rain, of sun and mist which the Indians believed to be hidden on Watchdog Mountain. But now they talked among themselves of another treasure to be found there, a treasure of furs which might be bought for mere trinkets and sold in Europe for money. And this money might buy better food and clothing for the men's families, giving them leisure to lead better lives and bringing security against want.

One of the men smiled and pointed at the mountain. The vision of wealth which he had glimpsed caused him to look more closely at the mountain whose beaver might make his dream come true. As he looked he noticed something he had not seen before.

"Look," he said, "the mountain looks like an old dog. There is his back and there is the friendly old face."

"You are right," agreed another. "The mountain looks like an old watchdog guarding our treasure of furs. I hope he will not prove a surly, snapping dog when we take away the treasure."

The men laughed and then became silent. They were thinking perhaps about the hard struggle that lay ahead in this new country. They did not yet know about its strange plants and animals, fierce storms, cold winters and burning summers.

They looked at the men who had come in the canoes, standing beside them, and wondered if these men would remain as friendly as they were then. For a moment some of the newcomers felt a little shiver of doubt as they thought of the obstacles to be overcome on their pathway to riches. It seemed to them the mountain had grown larger and that the old dog now looked at them as if listening and preparing to spring at them in anger.

But this was for only a moment. Soon they were laughing together again, for they knew well that the mountain could know nothing of their plans or hopes. They knew that mountains cannot feel or hear or know, for they are made of hard rock and not of flesh and bone and nerve.

One of the men raised his arm and shook a fist at the shadowy blue mountain. "Lie still, you old dog!" he shouted. "Don't try to frighten us away. For nothing can stop us now! We are going to become rich men, and if you don't like that – well, it doesn't matter!"

# 3

# Trader's Treasure

The European ship sailed out of the shadow of the mountain and down the river. The Indians watched from the bank and tried hard not to show their sadness at seeing the wonderful ship returning to the mysterious land from which it had come.

But soon another ship, sent by the owners of the first, anchored

13

at the mouth of Watchdog Creek. The Indians saw the new people land and begin to cut trees and build a log trading post.

The Indians showed them the best places to fish and what plants could be eaten and which ones were dangerous. They told them about the seasons in the valley and the forest and about the animals.

When the post was completed and stocked with trade goods, Kit Holmes, the sharp-eyed trader, tempted the Indians with his iron axes, red cloth, warm blankets, beads, knives and guns.

"Bring me all kinds of furs," Holmes urged. "Bring mink and otter and wildcat – but be sure to bring me plenty of beaver. I'll give more beads and finer cloth and sharper knives for beaver skins than for any other. For the beaver is king of all fur-bearing animals."

There was a good reason why the trader urged the Indian hunters to bring him beaver. In Europe beaver fur was greatly sought after. A way had been found of removing the soft shorter hairs from beaver skins and making a fine felt from them. And this felt was used to make the strongest and lightest and most handsome of hats. A craze for beaver hats had swept Europe. Many a man was doing without things he badly needed in order to be able to buy an expensive beaver hat like the one worn by the king or leader whom he admired and followed. For a hat was no longer just an object to cover the head. It had become a symbol of faiths and loyalties and hopes.

At first the Indians were not so sure they should bring the skins that trader Holmes urged them to bring. For a close tie of friendship and respect  bound the native people to the beaver. As children they had watched by night and wondered at the way communities of beaver worked together felling trees with their teeth and making dams of the trunks and branches. They had marveled at the beaver's skill in building strong houses in the safety of the ponds behind the dams, and at his cleverness in placing the door of his house deep under water where no beaver-hungry wolverine could enter.

# Treasure of Watchdog Mountain

They knew that beaver were kind and devoted to their young ones. They were brave and resolute when faced with danger, yet calm when they saw that death was inevitable. They were industrious, neat and wise. And above all, the beaver were wonderfully kind to humans. Their skins gave them warm garments; their bodies furnished food. Their paddle-shaped tails supplied the most delicious dish to be served at a feast.

They took great care to avoid offending the spirits of the animals whose bodies gave them materials for food or clothing so these gifts would not be withheld in the future. And they took unusual pains to keep from giving offense to the kindly beaver spirits. They had always buried or sunk in the river the bones of the beaver they ate, lest their dogs might gnaw them and therefore displease the proud spirits. They made pets of young beaver, who ran about their villages, where the children treated them as brothers and played at making dams in their houses.

But when parents saw the eyes of their children shining as they stared at the trader's wonders, as the men heard their wives joyfully exclaim at the ease with which they could sew with the trader's metal needles, their doubts disappeared. No longer did they worry about the beaver spirits. Many of them trapped and shot, forgetting their own ways and old skills in their eagerness to bring beaver skins to the trading post.

The Indians were dazzled by the prospect of freedom from hard labor which the iron tools promised to bring. Surely, they thought, these magical tools – the guns, the knives, the traps, the shovels, the chisels and axes – will bring us long days of plenty and luxury. And so – dreaming of a better life to come for themselves and their families – they camped out in the caves of the lower slopes of Watchdog Mountain and pursued the beaver.

16

# Trader's Treasure

The old men muttered warnings. "Let us take care not to hurt the beaver spirits," they said. "Already we have seen the bones of beaver carelessly thrown aside to be gnawed by the village dogs. Already we have heard disrespectful words spoken by trappers which might give offense to the beaver spirits and even to the gods on Watchdog Mountain."

Not long after, harsh changes came. The high price the beaver skins brought led white trappers and hunters to compete with the Indians along the streams where the beaver were plentiful. A settlement called Trader's Landing grew up around the trading post, and from here newly-arrived farmers began pushing out into the valley. They elbowed out the Indian farmers from the choice fields along Watchdog Creek. They acted surprised and grieved when when anyone protested. Indians and white men often argued and sometimes fought.

Another change was the worst of all. The beaver, once so plentiful, became hard to find. For beaver are unable to endure the strain of continual pursuit. Soon there were none left of all the multitudes that had once lived and worked in the streams that flowed down from the old mountain.

The Indian hunters now found that trader Holmes did not smile at them as freely as before. He drove a harder bargain with them for skins of mink and wildcat, for he knew that the hunters were in his power. Many of them had become dependent upon him and the other newcomers. They had lost their old ways and had come to regard the their tools and cloth and foods as necessities of life.

Bitterness and resentment showed in the peoples' faces and actions. Their neighbors had taken away their cornfields and hunting grounds, and in exchange given them only a dream of happiness from

17

which they were awakening in pain and sorrow. Then the trader urged them to take his strong drink in exchange for their furs – the drink that had the power to make them feel merry for a time, even in the midst of sorrow. More and more the Indian hunters came away from the trading post with only drink and without food or cloth for their families.

Quarrels became more frequent and burst into war. The Indians raided farms and villages, killing the invaders of their soil and driving away their cattle. The Europeans replied by driving the Indians from the valley and destroying their villages. Perhaps, some Indians thought, they were being punished. They had turned against the friendly beaver; they had forgotten their gods.

Soon the new settlers spread out over the valley to the base of Watchdog Mountain. They cut and burned trees and planted crops among the blackened stumps. But before long, an enemy appeared to plague them. The mountain's forests were the home of animals who crept down by night to eat the farmer's crops and steal his stock. Raccoons came to eat cherries, bears and squirrels to eat young ears of corn, deer to nibble the buds from young fruit trees, and foxes and wolves to take chickens and little pigs.

The farmers trapped and hunted the animals. Often they came to town with their backs bowed under the weight of the skins they were taking to the trader's. But the animals kept on coming. They were attracted by smells of new and more delicious foods than any the Indians had grown.

Jacob Morley, who was building up a fine farm on the old beaver meadows along Watchdog Creek, brought his neighbors together to stage drives against squirrels, deer and wolves. Men and boys stationed here and there on the mountain came together at a signal, ringing cowbells, shouting and lighting fires to drive the animals to a place where they could be easily shot or driven into the wilderness behind the mountain.

In spite of the farmers' war against them, the animals only increased in number. For they were well fed, and close by was the friendly refuge of Watchdog Mountain. There the hunted animals could find safety while men and dogs clambered in confusion over the tangled fallen trunks and branches that littered the ground under the great mossy trees. The animal community on Watchdog was strong. It would take more than the firing of a few guns, or the barking of a few dogs, to harm it.

While the valley farmers were building homes and fighting the mountain's animals, far away in the city that had sprung up at the point where the quiet river meets the sea, men who had never seen Watchdog were talking. Lawyers' clerks sitting on their high stools were drawing up long documents full of "whereas's" and "to wit's," in which the name of Watchdog Mountain occurred over and over again.

Businessmen were stopping other businessmen on the streets and carrying on long conversations in which the name of the mountain could be heard. Contracts were being signed, money was changing hands, men were studying maps and marking the spot where Watchdog Mountain stands.

All this bustling came about because a new treasure had been discovered on the mountain. This treasure was nothing less than the living forest coat which protected the animals and held the soil and water of the mountain.

A mighty blow was about to be struck at the old Watchdog. It would require the united efforts of many men over many years. It would scar the mountain deeply and bring desolation to its thriving plant and animal community.

*"Who can own a tree?"*
often attributed to Sitting Bull

# 4
# GLASSMAKER'S TREASURE

B en Sims hated trees. Wherever he went he was miserable until every tree around was cut down. Old Canfield, who was one of the men working under Sims at the clearing on the bank of the river near Watchdog, claimed he knew why Sims felt that way.

"The boss has good cause to hate trees," said Canfield as he and the other woodcutters were taking a brief rest on a newly felled pine log. "Ever wonder how he got that lame arm and the scar across his cheek? Well, they were given him by the very same old beech tree that killed his father when the two of them were cutting it down on their farm. Both of them knew how to handle a tree well enough. But this one seemed to have the devil in it. Instead of falling the way it should, it chased right after the two Sims with murder in its eye, so to speak."

# Treasure of Watchdog Mountain

The other men nodded grimly. They had all known trees like that. Most of them had a scar somewhere or a stiff back or a missing toe, thanks to a blow from a falling tree or a cut from an axe that had slipped for no good reason.

"Who doesn't hate trees?" asked the youngest of the men. "They stand between us and prosperity. They take up the good earth that ought to be growing fine crops of wheat or corn or pasturing cattle. Before a man can have a field he has to cut down so many trees and clean up so many stumps that he's too worn out to care whether he has a farm, or not. I tell you, trees are the worst enemy we have in this state, now that the Indians are taken care of. Come on boys, let's get after them." And he grabbed his axe and got to work.

It was not only because he hated trees that Ben Sims whistled so cheerily as he watched the pine trees falling under the axes of his men that April morning. For ahead, at the end of the road which he was about to build across the valley and aimed right at the heart of Watchdog Mountain, there waited the glittering possibility of riches, honor and security for Ben and his partners, the city businessmen. That possibility existed because America was no longer a new land, but was growing up.

Not many years had passed since the United States had become a free and independent nation. Americans had begun the hard task of building an independent national life. They had begun to do for themselves many things which had formerly been done for them by the mother country. American industry was growing and spreading.

Sims' partners had risked a large sum of money in men's wages, materials and equipment in the hope of profiting by supplying one of their country's needs. They proposed to use the treasure of trees which covered Watchdog in making one of the commonest, but most needed, of everyday substances. This substance was glass.

22

# Glassmaker's Treasure

They were sending Sims to Watchdog because there, close to a river which could furnish cheap and easy transportation for raw materials and finished products, was an immense forest. This wood was a great source of fuel. The trees were of the kind best suited to provide the tremendous heat glass-making needed. It would be difficult to haul the sand and other materials used to make new glass up the mountain and then transport the finished glass back down the mountain. It took nearly a month of stoking the fire to get a furnace up to heat. But there were more trees than anyone could imagine.

Sims quickly showed he was the right man for the job. In a few weeks he had a wharf and some log buildings ready on the river bank and was making a start on the road to the mountain. Soon the road was winding like a snake past corn and wheat fields near well-built farmhouses, past log cabins standing in lonely stump-dotted clearings, and over brooks and swamps.

# Treasure of Watchdog Mountain

After many days of hard work, Sims and his men plunged into the dark forests along the base of Watchdog Mountain. Here men sweated and oxen panted, for the going was hard among great trees and rocks fallen from the ledges above. But the road moved on. It slipped by under the Watchdog's nose and followed the course of a hurried stream that raced down the side of the mountain.

Beside a waterfall in the stream, Sims ordered his men to stop. For the road had reached its goal at this lonely spot on a narrow plateau in the midst of a wilderness. There was no rest for Sims and his men. At once they attacked the beech, maple and hemlock trees growing large and close together.

They built a rough little sawmill and sawed some of the trees into planks. Workers dug clay from the stream bank and molded and burned it into bricks. With these they built furnaces and chimneys for the long glasshouses which the carpenters were putting up. A row of little cabins sprang up amid the stumps. When the cabins were finished, the wives and children of the workers arrived and found a little schoolhouse waiting for them and a store with hams and dried fish, calico, slates and needles on its shelves.

Here was a new community to join the older one of plants and animals on the mountain. It was small and weak. It formed only a strange little island in a great sea of leaves, tied to the rest of the human world by nothing but the thin faltering line of the road to the river.

But already this human community was coming into conflict with the mountain's older inhabitants. Ben Sims found that out beyond any shadow of a doubt when the long hot spell came near the end of August.

Things had been going badly for a week or two, as was made plain by the fact that Sims had ceased to whistle as he directed his men. For half the people in the glassmaker's village were lying in their cabins sick with chills and fever. Many more, weakened by illness, stumbled through the day without accomplishing anything.

# Glassmaker's Treasure

Sims muttered and growled, for he knew that every day the opening of the factory was delayed cost him and his partners a great deal of money. In his confident way he had contracted with expert glassblowers who were already arriving and being paid high wages although there was nothing for them to do – nothing but to lie down and shiver and burn through the hot August days.

It was clear to Sims that his partners would not pay money to keep the village going unless there was a prospect of a quick profit. Maddened, he roused workers from their beds and tried to drive them to pick up axes and hammers and to put the yokes on their oxen again. But the weak, yellow-faced men could not move, even when driven by Sims' scornful words.

Sims took off his coat and seized a hammer. He banged away in the unfinished factory building. His men smiled, even in their sickness, at the awkwardness of their boss's weak arm. In disgust Sims threw down the hammer and strode off. He looked at the tangle of tree trunks and branches scattered around the village and imagined he saw evil faces leering at him from the trees' gnarled branches and reaching threatening arms toward him.

For Sims knew that the illness which now seemed about to wreck his hopes was in some way connected with trees. It seemed to attack the people of frontier communities just as they had made a good start at felling trees and building their houses.

Yes, Sims thought, trees are my enemies. Even when they are lying dead on the ground they have the power to harm me, as if in revenge because I ordered them cut down.

Sims was right in thinking that there was a connection between the cutting of trees and the disease called "chills and fever," although no one was to know for many years what that connection was. But the explanation, when it came, was simple. Certain kinds of mosquitoes, which cause malaria, find conditions in new

25

clearing very much to their liking. There they multiply in the hot, late summer months, emerging from hiding to feast on human blood by night.

The joining of the Watchdog Mountain society by human beings was having many effects on the plants and animals – the mosquitoes were but one of many. But Ben Sims, who had succumbed to chills and fever himself, knew nothing of all this. He tossed on the hard bed in his little cabin, swearing wildly at the forest and the Watchdog, and in his delirium making extravagant boasts about the terrible fate he planned for the mountain's trees when he should recover.

The first frosts of early October brought relief to the weary little village. The mosquitoes ceased to bite and slowly some of the sick began to recover. But the people of the glassmaker's village had been hard hit and for a long time they remained weak. Before the long cold winter that followed was over, a row of tombstones stood on a knoll near the factory showing that in their fight for the mountain's treasure, the glassmakers had lost the first battle.

But though this battle had been lost, trees and mountains cannot hold out for long against human determination and energy and the power that lies in their inventions of tools and money. A year and a half after he had begun his clearing on the property on the river bank, Sims opened his factory for business.

Wood was thrown into the furnaces and the fires were lit. From that moment on, day after day, the fires burned on as grimy stokers working in relays fed log after log to the white hot flames.

Through the cool months of the year, gangs of woodsmen brought down beech, maple and oak trees on the mountainside. Often they worked knee-deep in snow, their faces tormented by biting winds. Other men split the tree trunks and piled them up to season. Still others hauled them, with yokes of oxen, to the factory where they were dried in ovens before being used.

All these men worked to keep the furnaces of the glass factory blazing ceaselessly with a heat intense enough to melt the sand of which glass is largely made. And each tree cut on Watchdog Mountain spent all the energy it had gathered in its lifetime in one brief burst of fiery power, before becoming ashes on the furnace floor and smoke and gas blown across the mountainside by the wind.

Ben Sims whistled once again. For he saw his men felling trees. He saw the glassblowers hard at work, and boxes of window glass and bottles creaking down to the river in ox carts to be loaded on boats and sent to market. The prospect that he would certainly overcome the losses of the first year and make a huge profit seemed certain.

But there was one thing that Sims had overlooked, and that was the greediness of the glass furnaces for wood. He had taken it for granted that there would be enough trees of the right kind available for an indefinite period. But after ten moderately prosperous years, he noticed that all the trees within easy reach of the factory were gone. It was beginning to take a great deal more time and more hours of work to bring each load of wood to the factory than it had in the early days. The woodsmen began cutting trees which they had left standing at first because they were too small. They began mixing the less desirable softwoods, such as hemlock and pine, with the hard woods.

A change in Ben Sims began to be noticed by his men. No longer did he speak of trees with hatred. When, in the course of his endless wandering over the Watchdog's sides in search of trees, he found a good stand or a tree starting to sprout, he expressed his whole-hearted happiness. He was even known to slap a fine beech on its trunk and exclaim, "Look at that tree, boys. Isn't she a beauty?"

The growing shortage of wood was not Sims' only worry. Glass factories located in other parts of the country were beginning to use a new fuel – coal – and were able to sell glass for less than the Watchdog Mountain Glass Company. Sims' city partners read his reports and grumbled. They had invested a lot of money in the factory. For some years they had lost steadily before beginning to make a modest profit. Now they were losing again, with little chance of ever regaining their losses.

His partners told Sims they had had enough of glass-making. They ordered him to close the factory before it left them penniless. So, after many years of activity, the fires of the glass factory on Watchdog Mountain were allowed to go out. A few of the workers remained to farm on the best of the land cleared by the woodsmen, but most of the glassmakers left their village forever.

Blackberry bushes grew in the streets. Porcupines and mice gnawed at the empty buildings. Swallows nested in the doorless cabins. Green and gray molds and mosses began to collect on floors and walls to do their work of reducing the buildings to earth once more.

Ben Sims, who had suddenly become an old man after the failure of the scheme in which he had poured so much work and energy, went to Trader's Landing to live with his son, a bright young lawyer already being mentioned as the next county judge.

Sims spent his days with the other old men and the idle young ones sitting on the porch of the Drover's Inn chewing tobacco, whittling and talking. There was one piece of advice he liked to give to the younger men, and indeed, to anyone who would listen.

"See that mountain over there?" Sims would say, pointing to the west. "That's the old Watchdog. Now, once when I was young and full of nonsense, I was fool enough to pick a fight with that mountain. Take my advice, young feller, and when you're just spoiling for a fight, pick on something your own size and don't take on a mountain. Because you'll get the pants licked offa you. Yessir – you sure will."

*"A picture is a poem without words."*
Confucius

# 5
# ARTIST'S AND TANNER'S TREASURE

The people of Trader's Landing understood most strangers who came along. They understood the drovers with their cattle, the rogues with schemes for getting other people's money, the businessmen with an eye out for an honest dollar, and the rest of the travelers who came up or down the river. But this fellow James Barton – he was a puzzler.

It wasn't that he wasn't a good artist. The portraits he painted of the Landing people were fine likenesses. But why did he sit on rocks and logs in all kinds of weather making sketches of Watchdog Mountain? What a waste! American scenery was nothing for an artist to bother with. What ought to inspire him were ruined castles, English meadows or ivy-covered cottages – what you could see in picture books. But an American mountain or valley just meant hard work and the chance to make some money. Nothing romantic about that.

After Barton had packed up and left Trader's Landing, people went on shaking their heads when he was mentioned. But the time came when the head shaking stopped – to be replaced by a look of respect. That was after the piece appeared in the big city paper. Everybody in the Landing read it over and over.

"The sensation of the moment," they read, "is a painting called 'The Old Watchdog' which has just been placed on exhibition here. In it the artist James Barton has tried to paint a truly American landscape and has succeeded. Here is a mountain with its cliffs and trees and the clear sunlit sky above it – all as American as the Indians themselves and as beautiful as anything old Europe has to offer.

"And what is more, there is something novel about the image which draws thousands to see it. When looked at steadily for a time, the mountain seems to change and become an old dog lying down on guard over the valley below. The painter, his painting, and the remarkable mountain are likely to become famous. An engraving of it is being made. It is expected to become enormously popular."

After reading this and seeing the engraving, the Landing people took a good look at their mountain. It was the same old watchdog they knew, and yet it seemed different now. Their eyes were opened to

a new way of seeing their own land. For the first time, they saw the beauty of the old mountain.

A year later a new and larger boat was added to the line of white and gold river steamboats that brought people from all parts of America who wanted to see the Watchdog with their own eyes. The name of the Drover's Inn in Trader's Landing was soon changed to The Watchdog

31

# Treasure of Watchdog Mountain

Hotel. Guests were driven to Artist's Rock, from which Barton was said to have made the sketches for his painting. Valley farmers added rooms to their houses and advertised in the city papers for guests to spend a few weeks in the romantic "Watchdog Mountain Country."

Guests arrived in large numbers. They wore a trail up the mountain and carved their initials on the topmost ledge. Young ladies gathered plants on the mountainside and pressed them in albums to show how well they understood the fashionable hobby of botany. Others wandered in the woods to study the wild animals and the rocks or to admire the beauty of the waterfalls.

Down in town, folks wondered how they could profit from the fact so many wanted to see Watchdog Mountain. A group of businessmen announced a plan. They would build the most splendid mountain house right on top of the old Watchdog. It would have thick carpets, gold-framed mirrors, soft beds, fine food, music, dancing and sermons. Shares in the enterprise would be sold. The profits, to those farseeing enough to buy, might well be enormous.

Twenty miles up the river another group of men had other ideas. They had heard that fortunes were being made in tanning hides using the tannin in which the bark of hemlock trees is rich. Both of the Watchdog's sides were covered with fine hemlock forests. These hemlocks would keep a tannery going for only three or four years, the men estimated. But in that time they could make a nice profit. They outbid the men who had made plans for the new hotel, and Watchdog and its treasure of hemlock bark became their property.

At once they set to work. They built a ragged set of buildings in what came to be known as Tannery Hollow. Their men swarmed over the mountain during the late spring and early summer when the hemlock bark was easily removed from the trees. The great mossy trunks crashed to the ground by the thousands. Quickly the bark was stripped and the trees left where they had fallen.

The barkpeelers' life was not easy. Often they muttered that the Watchdog was fighting back at them. But the work went on. They struggled with swarms of tiny biting gnats. They sometimes jumped as they heard the whir of a rattlesnake close to their feet. The sticky hemlock sap covered their faces and hands and clothing. They stuck to trees and branches. Their hands stuck together. Sometimes two men stuck to each other and had to be pulled apart.

Three years later it was all over. A dozen men had been killed or crippled by falling trees. A hundred of the horses which hauled the bark from the woods and the hides to and from the river boats had been worn out and sold for what their hides and bones would bring. Thousands of Americans, and other people all over the world, wore breeches or shoes made from leather tanned on Watchdog Mountain.

When the accounts were settled, the tanners found that they had made a fair profit – $58,089.23. One of them had a fine gold pin made for his wife with part of his share. It was shaped like the Watchdog, with a diamond marking the spot where the abandoned tannery buildings stood.

The tanners had done well, but it was quite another story with the mountain. Wherever on its sides hemlock trees had grown, there was now a network of trunks and branches bleaching in the sun. Some

# Treasure of Watchdog Mountain

boys from the valley claimed that they had walked for miles on the fallen trees without once touching their feet to the ground. The boys reported, too, that the path to the top was choked with dead branches. They said that the waterfalls and wildflowers had dried up in the fierce sun that beat on them now that the shading hemlocks were gone.

Fewer people stayed at the Watchdog Hotel or visited Artist's Rock. Some farmers who had done well keeping boarders went back to raising oats and corn.

Many people said that it was too bad that the old Watchdog had been treated so roughly by the tanners. But they all agreed that there was nothing anybody could do about it. The tanners had bought and paid for the mountain. What they did with their property was their business and nobody else's.

*"The creation of a thousand forests is in one acorn."*
Ralph Waldo Emerson

# 6
# The Fire

On his farm near the tannery, Isaac Gilmore stood outside the kitchen door before breakfast one October morning and looked across the pasture to his upper lot. Since the glass-makers had cut the beech and maple trees that had stood there, the lot had grown up to weeds and then to huckleberry bushes. These mixed with little saplings of birch and poplar. They grew all the way up to where the debris from criss-crossed hemlock trunks left by the barkpeelers began.

At breakfast Gilmore remarked to his wife that huckleberries were bringing a good price from the men who shipped them down the river to the big city. There had been plenty of huckleberries in the upper lot that summer, but they'd been a little small.

"There's nothing will improve a huckleberry patch like a good burning over," said Gilmore. "The mountain's dry as a bone this morning – looks like a good time to fix that upper lot."

So a little later Gilmore set the lot on fire. When he came back to the house he was enthusiastic. "Those flames are racing across the lot like a bunch of hungry calves at feeding time," he said. "I ought to get a good burn up there."

Later on there could be no doubt about it. Isaac Gilmore got a good burn – much more of a burn than he bargained for. But at first his fire seemed to be doing just what he had meant it to do. When it reached the high cliff that marked the end of the upper lot, it seemed to die out. And it did really die out – except for one little smoldering bit that dug into the thick layer of dead leaves at the base of the cliff.

That evening when Gilmore came up to admire the fine burn, he didn't notice a faint wisp of blue smoke curling up against the cliff. He didn't know that the fire from which the smoke came was burrowing its way along the base of the cliff, pushed along by a gentle but steady breeze from the valley. By the next afternoon the fire had reached the break in the cliff where a pile of dead hemlock trees lay sprawled on a slope covered with dry leaves.

Standing outside later that night, little Sarah Gilmore said, "I smell smoke. I really do."

36

# The Fire

All the Gilmores sniffed. Isaac opened the door and saw that the dead hemlock trees at the break in the cliff were ablaze. He remained calm. "If the breeze holds the way it is for a while, we won't have a thing to worry about," he said, "because by then the fire will be well up the mountain. There's nothing worth a lead shilling up there."

Afterwards, two ladies coming home from a prayer meeting at the Baptist church in Trader's Landing saw a small bright spot on the side of the Watchdog a little above the Gilmore farm. One of the ladies said that it might be somebody's lantern. The other asked what anybody in his senses would be doing up there with a lantern at that time of night.

An hour later Will Bemis, editor of the *Landing Gazette*, looked out of his window as he always did before going to bed. "Looks like a little fire up on the Watchdog," he said, coming away from the window. "Hope it doesn't get any bigger." Mrs. Bemis said she'd been told that all the dead hemlock trees on the mountain were bound to go up in smoke some day. "Plenty of people wish it would happen and get done with," she said.

That night the fire, which had reached the plateau above the cliff, slowly gained strength. A little after sunrise it began climbing up the mountain, gathering speed and energy as it moved along. Sometimes it leaped ahead to set dry hemlocks ablaze in a moment. Sometimes it stood still as if making ready for another leap. Sometimes it spread when burning logs rolled down slopes and tumbled over cliffs in showers of sparks which set new fires. Slowly, methodically, the fire ate its way through the

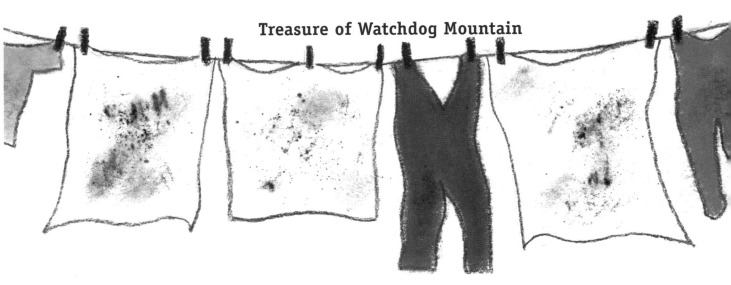

thick forest carpet, which was thoroughly dry now after long exposure to the hot rays of the sun.

Day after day it moved on. Soon a great cloud of smoke hid the mountain and rolled across the valley. When it reached the quiet river, the smoke flowed toward the sea. Ships moved slowly through air that seemed to form a white choking wall around them.

When Mrs. Bemis went out to bring in her washing she saw that all her clean sheets were specked with bits of black ash from the burning mountain. Old people chatting with neighbors coughed. Some people felt afraid and said they wondered if the whole world was going to burn up. More people than usual found their way to the Landing churches that Sunday and joined in their minister's prayers for rain to end the fire.

Behind the wall of smoke that seemed to have imprisoned the old Watchdog, flames licked and played. Hot air quivered upward. Leaves shriveled before becoming flashes of fire. Fire followed the fallen hemlock logs as if they were roads laid down for it to travel.

A few bears who had found berries and other food plentiful in the brush-filled areas left by the glassmakers fumbled while trying to find a path to safety. Flying sparks singed their fur. Mice and rabbits, puzzled by the smoke, the snapping of burning twigs, the heat and the

## The Fire

roaring of the fire scurried and stopped, then scurried again, some to safety, others to die. Insects crawled out from snug burrows in logs and then crawled back to await whatever might happen.

Hour after hour, day after day, the fire moved on. It explored crevices in the rocks, hunted out and destroyed piles of rotting brush left by the glassmakers. It withered the fresh new shoots pushing up from oak and maple stumps. In the intensity of the heat focused upon its cliffs, flakes and slabs of stone flew from the rocks and whirled down the mountain.

The people in the valley tried to stop the flames only when they threatened a neighbor's house or farm buildings along the mountain's base. They thought the treasures the mountain had held for them were now all gone. There was nothing left worth saving.

But even while the fire raged at its hottest, help was on its way. A great mass of cool moist air was moving across the country, coming closer each day. It arrived early one morning in a gust of wind that sent the flames dancing higher than ever. Raindrops pattered down gently and slowly. They turned to vapor in the heat and never even touched the flames. All that day clouds moved over the mountain and raindrops fell now and then. Still, the fire burned.

The rain hit, and hit hard, at sundown. Drops hissed as they struck warm rocks, sputtered as they touched flames, sizzled on burning wood. They no longer came down in drops, but in ragged sheets. It rained steadily for two days and then the sun rose in a clear and cool sky.

People looked up at the Watchdog that fall morning and exclaimed at how much it had changed. Here and there some trees still lived. A patch of spruces peeped over its back. A few groups of oaks and chestnuts stood near the tannery. But the old mountain seemed to have become a blackened desert. Old Mr. Maynard summed up what people thought when he said, "They say every dog has his day. Looks like the Watchdog has had his'n. He looks about through."

Winter came early that year. A few weeks after the fire had ended, the first flakes of snow came down on the mountain's back. By early December the mountain's scars were covered with a thick white coat on which lines and streaks of trees and rocks showed like dark markings on white fur. People felt better when they saw the old mountain looking almost gay and pretty in a new coat of snow. But they would not have felt that way had they known that every flake that fell on the Watchdog's back was to have a bitter meaning for them and for all the valley.

What that meaning was, no one was to know until spring.

# 7
# SPRING RAIN

A man can climb Watchdog Mountain all the way from Gilmore's Swamp up Tannery Hollow and over Indian Cave Trail to the top in a little over three hours – if he doesn't loiter too long to admire the view from Porcupine Rock.

It should take spring about two weeks to make the same climb. But even though it never stops to admire views, spring is an unpredictable climber.

In theory the winter snow on the lowest part of the mountain melts and runs off first. As the line of spring moves higher day by day, the water from the melted snow is fed into its streams a little at a time.

The spring that arrived after the fire didn't stick to the rules. It should have reached the base of the mountain a day or two after it came to Trader's Landing. Instead, cool air moving down from the north stopped it in its tracks.

# Spring Rain

For more than a week winter clung to the valley and mountain and even held the strong spring sun at bay. Then in a great rush of warm air and warm rain, spring leaped across the valley and halfway up the Watchdog's sides in a few hours.

The snow on the lower half of the mountain became softened by the warm air and worn down by the trickling raindrops. It melted and more rain came down.

For all the thousands of years during which its sides had been covered with a living coat, spring rain and melted snow had run off the mountain's sides fairly slowly. Not this time.

The heavy hemlock boughs that had broken the force of pelting rain and shaded the snow beneath were gone. Gone too were most of the fallen, decaying trunks and branches which could form little dams to restrain the water's energy. There was little left of the thick leaf and needle carpet to absorb and hold water. The tunnels and holes made by many earth-loving creatures were too crushed and choked to lead water to below the surface.

There was only a barren mountainside down which water could leap and tumble in unfettered response to the pull of the Earth's gravity.

Single drops of water met and joined to become larger ones. These drops became trickles. The trickles formed tiny streams which found an easy path downward along the rough paths and roads made by glassmakers and barkpeelers. Thousands of these little streams poured into the mountain brooks which raced faster and faster toward the valley, the river and the sea.

As the earth thawed, moving water tore at it. Grains of sand and soil were rushed to the brooks that were already dark with

bits of charred wood, mud, sticks and stones. Large rocks loosened by the pressure of the brooks rolled along with the water. Earth from undermined banks slid into the brooks. The air of the mountain vibrated with the roaring and splashing, with the grinding together of rocks and the gusty violence of the wind.

People watched with satisfaction – at first – as the water of Watchdog Creek began to rise. Old Mr. Maynard, who was wise in the ways of seasons and weather, hobbled down to take a look. He said to the Littlefield boys who were skipping stones on the swollen creek, "When you see the first robin or the first skunk cabbage comes up, maybe you're fooled. But when the snow melts offen the Watchdog's back and the creek rises high as the Widow Holmes' pear tree the way it's doing right now, then, by cracky, you've got spring."

But the water did not stop at the old pear tree. It rose higher as it washed out the yellow rose bush at the widow's back door. It invaded streets. It filled wells and cellars. It gushed into Mrs. Bemis' kitchen just as she was putting a roast of lamb into the oven. Mrs. Bemis ran for safety with the roast in her hands.

The floodwater seized everything that was loose. It upset some things. It turned others around. It carried a variety of objects to the river. Away went the red wagon standing beside the Littlefield's barn. Away went the chicken house John Van Alsten had built that winter. The people of the Landing abandoned their town and fled to the hills for safety.

Halfway between the mountain and the racing river, Fred Bailey, the miller, stood helplessly and watched his tall new mill wheel go to pieces under the battering of the logs and stones hurled against it by the flood. Farmers saw their fields covered deep with stones and gravel from the mountain as the creek bed filled with silt and overflowed.

Hiram Morley stood in the pounding rain and looked at the ten-acre field where he and his father had long grown the finest wheat in the county. Morley was a strong man who could take hard luck in his stride. But when he saw his pet field turned to a rocky, sandy waste, and the land beyond gouged and gullied, he came close to crying.

At the end of three days, the rain stopped and the sun shone brightly. The people of the Landing went back to clean and repair their homes. Women put soaked furniture and bedding to dry in the warm sunshine. Farmers mended buildings and fences and talked with each other about what to do with their damaged fields.

That spring the valley people were too busy to give much thought to their mountain neighbor. But when they did look up at it for a moment, they could not help noticing how gaunt and gray it had become.

Hardly a remnant of its fine living coat could be seen. Instead the surface seemed to be made up of a tattered and charred rag of soil with bony rocks pushing everywhere through the rents of the flood. The Sims boys, who had climbed up the mountain's sides to see what had happened there, reported it was uncannily quiet. They hadn't heard a single bird singing. There wasn't even a branch left for the wind to whistle in.

# Treasure of Watchdog Mountain

One fine morning that June, Hiram Morley and his family sat in their big wagon outside the farmhouse gate. Morley had become so discouraged by the damage to his fine farm that he had sold the place, lock, stock and barrel. Now he was off to the West where – so they said – the land was level as a parlor floor, and where the soil, untouched by man, was rich with the growth and decay of thousands of generations of prairie grass.

Eddy and Billy Morley had planned to give a great shout of "Hurrah – we're off for the West," as they started. But when their father tightened his fingers on the horses' reins and asked, "All ready?" the boys were silent and only nodded as they clung to their mother's hand.

They looked back for the last time at their once cozy little house and its barns. They looked at the great dark mountain against which their house stood and which they had known as a neighbor all their lives.

"Giddy-ap!" shouted Hiram Morley. The sound echoed faintly from Old Watchdog's side. The horses plunged onward on the long road to the West.

# 8

# QUARRYMAN'S TREASURE

Disaster had struck Watchdog Mountain many times. Fires kindled by lightning and Indian fires escaping from the valley had sometimes crackled through the hemlock or beech forests. Spring floods following heavy rains had often filled the mountain streams until they overflowed their banks.

But never since life became well established on its sides after the last ice age, had flames or water destroyed so much of the Watchdog's coat of soil and living things and done so much damage in the valley. For the work of the glassmakers, the barkpeelers and of the trappers who had destroyed the beaver and their dams had made it easier for fire and flood to ravage the mountainside.

During the few weeks after the flood, the mountain looked dark, shrunken, and lifeless. But each living thing struggles endlessly to expand the limits of its own kind. Lifeless places seldom remain lifeless for long. At once, the work of re-weaving the mountain's coat began.

In its days of desolation, as in its days of prosperity, the old Watchdog had one constant visitor roaming over every cliff and slope and seeking out every hollow. This was the wind. And the wind never came without bringing gifts. For every one carried little seeds – seeds borne on delicate whirling wings, seeds carried on fluffy white parachutes, seeds spreading little sails to the wind.

In the mountain's most thriving days few of these seeds could find a foothold amid the busy community of life that crowded its sides. But now many wind-borne seeds of plants adapted to the burned-over soil. In the cracks of rocks, on earth newly laid bare by the flood or on almost bare rock itself, they sprouted and took root.

The wind did not work alone. Birds who had eaten fruits or berries in the valley sometimes left indigestible seeds on the mountain. Wandering animals brought seeds tangled in their fur. The mountain itself had more life left in it than had seemed possible. Seeds and roots which had escaped fire and flood soon tried growing under new conditions.

By the second summer after the flood, the green of young golden-rod, grasses, ferns and other low plants was beginning to cover the mountain's burned and flood-ravaged surfaces. Huckleberry shoots long overshadowed by tree neighbors sprang into life in the full sunshine. Groups of fire-scarred trees, or others with roots exposed by the washing away of the soil around them, unfolded leaves in a struggle to live.

# Quarryman's Treasure

In the shelter of the low plants, poplar, cherry and birch seedlings were gaining the strength that would enable them to shoot high above the plants that now nursed them. As the plants flowered, bees and other insects found them. When seeds ripened, chipmunks, mice, birds and other seed-eaters joined the rabbits and other leaf-eaters who had already come back to eat its plentiful low green plants.

Meat-eating animals arrived – foxes, wildcats and hawks – attracted by the leaf and seed eaters. A vital plant and animal society once again was coming into being, nourished by the meager soil left on the mountain.

Isaac Gilmore had been right in thinking that fire would improve the huckleberry crop by providing the sun the plants liked best. The berries in his upper lot and elsewhere on the mountain did so well that Gilmore prospered in the huckleberry business. Every summer he brought families from the valley to camp out and pick berries which he sold at a profit.

Now other men were also looking up at the mountain with interest. On its cool slopes, where sun-loving huckleberries did not thrive, the poplar, cherry and birch trees were being crowded out by maple, ash, beech and oak. These hardwood trees, the men in the valley told each other, would soon be big enough to be worth money.

The old Watchdog's new living coat was being made in an age when American bridges and railroad cars, fences, houses, ships, wagons and household tools were made of wood. Food was packed in wooden barrels or boxes. Locomotives and steamboats burned wood. Houses were warmed and cooking was done by wood fires. Roads were often paved with wooden planks. The men whose fathers had called trees their worst enemy now regarded a good stand of timber as a valuable thing.

The mountain's trees grew slowly, for they came from soil from

which much of the strength had been burned or washed away. But they grew day by day. Woodcutters began to cut the larger trees to sell for fuel. Isaac Gilmore's son Billy built a little factory in Tannery Hollow where he made chair legs, rolling pins and baseball bats from the wood of young ash and maples.

The activities of the woodcutters were only a small threat to the mountain's coat. There was a larger one, which carried danger not only to the mountain's coat, but to the whole mass of the mountain itself.

It had been discovered that the stone of which it was formed could easily be split into smooth slabs that were the best in all the country for sidewalks. As American cities rapidly expanded, the demand for this stone led Judge Sims' sons, Jack and Charley, to form a company for quarrying stone on the mountain. The prospects seemed good. The river would furnish cheap transportation to markets as it had done earlier for glass and furs. Many eager workmen clamored for jobs, even at low pay.

Not many years passed before the sides of the Watchdog were again streaked with the lines of rough roads. These led to quarries which showed like scars on the mountainside. Shabby quarrymen's villages sprang up where hard-working men and women tended gardens or fiddled and danced and played with their children after working hours.

Long lines of stone-laden wagons crawled over the dusty roads to the wharves at Trader's Landing. Old Judge Wilkins had to interrupt sessions of the county court from time to time as the wagons creaked and rumbled past, drowning out the arguments of attorneys and making the judge himself cough, as dust invaded the courtroom.

Jack and Charley Sims built themselves fine new houses – each with a tower – overlooking the river. They were the largest houses ever built in the Landing and served to show everyone that the quarries were profitable indeed. But some neighbors of the Watchdog worried a little as the quarries grew larger and more numerous.

Mrs. Evangeline Sullivan, who owned the Watchdog Glen Boarding House near the Landing, was one of the people who worried most. Her business had improved a little after the blows from the tanners, the fire and the flood. Now it seemed threatened again. Mrs. Sullivan wrote a letter to Editor Bemis of the *Landing Gazette*. She said she thought something should be done to keep the quarrymen from ruining the looks of the mountain. If the mountain should stop looking like a watchdog as it did in the painting, it might mean the end of the boarding business.

The editor wrote a reassuring editorial in answer to Mrs. Sullivan's letter. The stone of Watchdog Mountain, he wrote, was a great treasure which would bring employment and prosperity to the valley for many years. Even if some people should go elsewhere to spend their vacations, it wouldn't matter. Many more would come to live in the valley as the quarries grew.

He had consulted an authority on such matters, the editor said. He had learned that if quarrying went on at the same rate, it would take almost a thousand years to level Watchdog Mountain to the ground. "So," said the editor, "there is no cause for alarm – none at all."

# 9
# TREASURE OF WATER

ONCE again the old Watchdog seemed doomed.

Quarrymen, woodcutters and others, all doing what seemed right to them, threatened the mountain with total destruction. But when the mountain's future seemed darkest, help came again.

## Treasure of Watchdog Mountain

This help came from the Landing's serious young doctor, William Smith. "We are no longer a village here; we have become a city," the doctor said over and over again. "We need a good supply of pure water. Clean water will help us attain a level of comfort and health that is suitable for the people of this prosperous nation. And we need that water quickly, or we may have epidemics that will take many lives. Already, I have traced many ailments to our bad water."

Everyone agreed with the doctor, but one big problem stood in the way of getting that clean water. The river had become polluted by the many communities on its banks which allowed their sewage to flow into it. No way of making this water fit for use was then known. The only possible source of clean water was the upper part of Watchdog Creek. The side of the mountain on which the creek arose belonged to the Sims brothers, who had their quarries there. They would not permit the water to be used, for fear it would cut the profits from their quarry business. And their wealth had brought them so much influence and power that no one wanted to put any pressure on them.

But Dr. Smith was a stubborn man. He kept on fighting. He fought harder because he had a second reason – one which he did not talk about – for keeping up this struggle. He could never forget the dark spring morning when he arrived with his parents from England to make their home in the Landing. At first he had felt lonely and unhappy in this new land. But that morning as his river boat approached the Landing, young William looked up and smiled. For as he stared at the mountain he saw it losing its forbidding appearance. It was as if it took on the form of a friendly old dog ready to protect him from harm. From that moment, the boy felt safe and at home in America.

Often the doctor laughed at himself for having had such a child-ish feeling. "I am a scientific man living in a scientific age," he used to tell himself. "I have no business feeling this way about a mountain. After all, it is only a mass of cold hard rock, thinly covered with a soil which supports numerous plants and animals. It cannot feel; it cannot think. It doesn't know about William Smith, or of the needs of the city near it for the water which flows down its sides."

Yet the doctor came to believe that his childhood feeling toward the mountain had not been entirely wrong. For just as the old Watchdog had helped him, and in a way was his friend and protector, it was the friend and protector of all who lived in the valley. If they treated the mountain wisely, the doctor knew, it could give them water for the city. It could give all of them timber and animals for fur and food. It could give visitors a place to come to for vacations. More artists would come and find beauty in the mountain, and craftspeople could follow the artists. It could be a special place. "Yes," he con-cluded, "I shall go on thinking of Watchdog Mountain as my good friend and neighbor."

So the doctor went on talking to the people and writing to newspapers and to members of the government urging that Watchdog Mountain be made into a state park. He wanted it to be forever the property of the people. But those who worked in the quarries, store keepers, owners of river boats and many others whose liveli-hoods depended on the mountain quarries opposed him. Powerful Senator Holmes, a relative

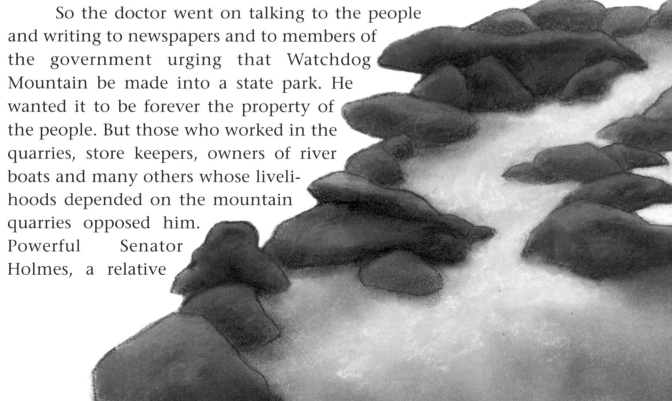

of the Sims brothers, could be depended upon to fight the doctor's plans in the state capital. But Dr. Smith never lost his faith that some day the city would get its water supply and the mountain would be safe.

Many years went by, and the doctor's beard turned gray before his chance finally came. Something happened then that threw Dr. Smith into a tremendous flurry of activity. A group of men who had been experimenting with new and cheap ways of making cement from limestone had been successful. Soon tunnels were being driven into another mountain down the river from the Watchdog. The rock was being treated with heat and converted into a cement which, when mixed with sand, could be used to make sidewalks. These cost a lot less than those made of Watchdog Mountain stone. The demand for Watchdog's stone diminished, then stopped.

The Sims brothers admitted defeat. They closed the quarries. Tall weeds shot up on the mountain roads so recently traveled by the stone-laden wagons. Dr. Smith organized a group of citizens to appear before a committee of the legislature. The doctor spoke eloquently and persuasively of the needs of his community and its relation to the mountain. He pointed out that other states, and the national government, too, had set aside tracts of land when it was felt this was the only way the interests of everyone would be safeguarded.

The doctor came home that night feeling quietly confident. "I noticed that Senator Holmes who is a member of the committee nodded as if in agreement several times as I spoke," the doctor told his wife at dinner. "And several members assured me that they will vote in favor of my proposal. Yes, I think that my patient, the old Watchdog, will recover yet."

*"Heaven is under our feet as well as over our heads."*
Henry David Thoreau

# 10
# Treasure for the Future

A few years after Dr. Smith had spoken to the committee of the legislature, the Watchdog passed into the keeping of all the people of the state. Since then many changes have taken place.

Many more people understand the problems of the mountain. They know that a tree can grow back again, but a rock will not return. There are laws prohibiting the destruction of trees and other plants. Laws regulate the hunting and trapping of animals. Laws defend against fire. Worn places in the old Watchdog's living coat have been mended. A vigorous plant and animal community has developed under the watchful eyes of men trained to understand the ways of living things and their relationship to humans. At the base of the mountain, a shining lake has been built from which water flows steadily to fill the needs of Trader's Landing.

The plant and animal community continues to change, as always. Slowly, as the forests return, the carpet on the ground deepens and the soil beneath becomes better able to hold water and to support living things. The hemlock and beech trees had, here and there, clung to a foothold in the moist soil on the mountain's trails and along its brooks. They now climb upwards as other plants prepare the way for them.

The huckleberry bushes which Isaac Gilmore tried to encourage are becoming scarcer and have fewer berries. For the trees soaring above them have cut out much of the light they need.

Leaf- and seed-eating animals have become plentiful since the growing forests have not yet crowded out too many of their food plants. Such meat-eaters as wolves have vanished or been greatly reduced in number by the valley farmers and hunters. But deer, after being hunted ruthlessly, have returned to the slopes. They would starve to death if they had to go high into the mountain's forests. They love a land with young trees and low-lying plants. But they also eat the flowers and ornamental trees in people's gardens.

There are foxes, coyotes, bobcats, raccoons, pheasant, grouse, fishers and turkeys. The black bear find plenty to eat in the garbage left by humans when they can't find enough berries in the mountains. Hunting of certain animals is permitted only during hunting season.

Along Watchdog Creek colonies of the beaver so much respected by the Indians are trying to raise their families. They are being protected and, at the same time, carefully watched lest they invade the valley and flood fields and homes with their ponds.

Sometimes you spot a soaring eagle high above, or a hawk as it swoops down to catch his prey; the old Watchdog is home to raptors, including goshawks, kestrels, osprey and other large birds, like ravens. You might step on a rattlesnake underfoot. Once the mountain was full of timber rattlers, but they had interfered with the farmers and were a menace to children. Folks still want to poach them, so the state watches this.

No longer does the community on Watchdog Mountain go its own way, as it once did, modified only by changes in temperature, moisture and sunshine. Man is now an intelligent, understanding member of the community. He has always been the strongest force in determining what would happen to the old mountain. Now, and in the future, his desires will be balanced with those of the animals and plants that live on and near Watchdog.

Man, like other living things, changes, and his wants and hopes and even his ideals change with him. It may well be that all of Watchdog Mountain's slopes will some day again carry dense forests like those so much hated by Ben Sims. Left in this way all of the mountain would serve to teach Americans what their country was like when first discovered by Europeans. It would be a place of recreation for everyone and a place where scientists could study the ways of living things.

It may also be that some day man's demand for timber or some other treasure will cause him to struggle once more with the old Watchdog. This seems unlikely. But if such a struggle were to take place again, it would be under careful supervision and control, rather than in the reckless way of past treasure hunters, thoughtlessly destroying for the sake of a quick and often small profit.

For the mountain now serves all the people, and will continue to do so as long as they understand how closely their welfare and that of their children is connected by uncountable ties with the destiny of the mountain. If they remain vigilant, the great treasure on Watchdog Mountain will be handed on to those who come after them – not diminished, but increased with use.

It is impossible when dealing with living things to look into the future. Some day the restless, curious, inventive human mind may find a way to make food and other needed materials directly from sunlight, water and minerals. Or they will find a way of supplying water to homes and farms without depending on large forest areas for collecting and storing. Or men may so change as to lose their need to seek understanding of their world and will no longer go to the forests and streams of their land for comfort and quiet. These things, and many more of which we cannot even dream, may alter the relationship between the valley people and their mountain.

But happen whatever may happen, the Watchdog and those who live in the valley beneath it are on good, friendly terms today. Joe Sims, grandson of quarry owner Jack Sims, has worked on a dairy farm in the valley ever since the last of his grandfather's fortune trickled

## Treasure for the Future

away. On fine mornings as Joe leaves his house for his employer's barn to take care of the milking, he is likely to look up cheerfully at the mountain above him and call out, "Hi, neighbor!"

The old Watchdog never returns Joe's greeting, for that is beyond the power of any mountain. But Joe goes on to his work as happily as if the mountain had actually called back to him. For he knows that there is now peace between men and mountain. He and the rest of the valley people and the old Watchdog are good neighbors and friends at last.

*"Going to the mountains is going home."*
John Muir

# About This Story

There wasn't a Mr. Sims, but many men cut, burned and slashed trees in the Catskill wilderness. This is a made-up story, or work of fiction. It tells about what really happened to one mountain, Overlook Mountain, but the characters and situations were invented by the author, Alf Evers.

Alf first wrote *Treasure of Watchdog Mountain* fifty-one years ago. He was the author of many children's books and an historian of the region. We worked with him on the new edition for a year and a half before he passed away. He told us this book inspired him to write his major history for adults, *The Catskills, From Wilderness to Woodstock.*

By studying the past, he said, we could learn from our mistakes and work to improve things for the future. He wanted today's young people to appreciate the precious heritage of the Catskill region he loved so much.

We changed as little as possible from Alf's original book. The first chapter updates geological information and the last chapter shows how the Catskill Mountains are different from the way they were when he

# About This Story

wrote it. We sought advice from experts and added paintings by artist Christie Scheele, who lives and hikes these mountains with her two children and her husband.

Alf lived on Overlook's slopes. The mountain has become one of the most popular of the Catskill peaks. Like most of the Catskill Mountains, it has been scarred many times and has recovered. Thousands of its beavers were killed and their fur made into hats. Millions of trees were cut down for glassmaking, tanning and furniture making. Huge slabs of the rock from which Overlook was formed were chiseled away to become the sidewalks people still walk on in New York and other cities.

Paintings, as Alf told us, helped people everywhere discover the beauty of the Catskill Mountains, America's first wilderness, and of the Hudson River, America's "first" river. Thomas Cole was the first of the early American Hudson River artists who became famous. He was followed by others like Frederic Church, who became a student of Cole's. These artists greatly respected the land, and they created the Hudson River School of painting. (This wasn't a real "school," but a way of depicting landscapes.) Overlook may have been painted more often than any other American mountain. Writers, musicians and artists have continued to come to these mountains for creative inspiration. Woodstock was home to two art colonies, Byrdcliffe and Maverick.

Overlook was repeatedly burned over the last 200 years. Alf's story talks about plans for a grand hotel – and a splendid mountain house on Overlook was built and burned down twice. Now residents and visitors hike to its ruins and to the fire tower nearby. And the shining lake in Alf's story – that was his made-up way of telling us the community got its clean water. Today, the Ashokan Reservoir provides water to New York City, and Cooper Lake Reservoir supplies the city of Kingston's water.

Conditions have improved in the Catskill Mountains but, once again, there are big challenges. One problem for all of New York state's mountains is acid rain from chemicals like sulfur, nitrogen, ozone and mercury. These are borne on the wind and come from industrial plants. They pollute the air for hundreds of miles. Their small particles drop into the water where fish and other organisms live, and birds and other wildlife drink this water.

More and more, people use the mountains for recreation. This is good as long as the environment isn't endangered or destroyed. People hike its many trails, fish in its streams, lakes and reservoirs, canoe and kayak, camp and ski. Everyone benefits — if the land and water are protected and respected. But trails can be dangerously eroded if they are over-used and not maintained. Then the soil washes away.

Many types of trees grow on Overlook today, which makes a healthy habitat. On top of Overlook are white birch, American elm, balsam fir, red spruce and mountain ash; American beech, eastern hemlock, sugar maples and red maples and red oaks grow on its slopes.

The summit is now part of the New York State Forest Preserve. You cannot harvest Overlook's timber or build on top of the mountain. By law it will remain "forever wild." But the state does not own all the land on the mountain, so a group of people formed the Woodstock Land Conservancy to protect the remaining higher elevations. To save it, they have bought more than 400 acres which has been added to the forest preserve. Sometimes, people donate their land. They put in their wills that when they die, their property should be kept for all the people.

Over the years there have been others like Dr. Smith who saw the destruction and tried to stop what was wrong. But they were few. Today, however, there are many voices, and information is shared.

There are not that many farms left, but people who have moved here from the city still work the earth in their gardens. Another problem is non-native plants from far away that are introduced by accident. The plants repollinate and crowd out the native plants. Scientists from different places research the plants and also examine new insect pests

# About This Story

that have invaded the forests because of climate or because they have been carried here in pieces of wood. (Without knowing it, travelers sometimes bring these pests with them on planes, in cars, or, even in their backpacks.)

Today, when a tree disease breaks out in another state, an expert there tells the expert in the Catskills to look out for trouble. An outbreak of sudden oak death syndrome hitting California's red oaks is a warning to watch the red oaks on Overlook.

We hope this kind of understanding continues.

Alf said: "I see living forms in nature that relate to the nature of man. We have to live together and understand one another. We have asked so much of the earth, but there are limits. We must continue to help the earth, and it will continue to be helpful to us."

The beauty and resources of these forests and wild places, open spaces and wetlands are unique. The Catskill Mountains are for all people of all ages, for all seasons, and for all time.

*Arthur and Jo Schwartz*

# Questions
# to Answer

In this book the humans, the animals, even the tiniest insect, the tall trees and smallest plants – all the living things – depended upon one other. Name some animals that eat other animals. What are some plants that offer protection to animals?

The first people of the Catskills were the Esopus Indians (one of the bands of the Munsee-Delawares, and in their language, Delawares are called Lenape). Imagine that you were a Lenape boy or girl whose father met Henry Hudson's *Half Moon* coming up the river. What would you want to know about these strange people?

Pretend you are an eleven-year-old child living five hundred years ago. Keep track of everything you would do over three days. In what ways would your life be different from today?  How might your life be similar?

What Native American traditions are still alive in this region?

What crops did farmers grow in the fertile valleys of the Catskill Mountains?

Are there animals that once lived in your area, but no longer do? What happened to them?

# Questions to Answer

Can you name a mountain, lake, river, or area near you? What can you find out about its history?

Do you know what your area looked like 100 years ago? Do you know what it looked like 200 years ago? Do you know what it looked like after the last ice age?

Can you name 10 living things that are found in the river, lake or pond nearest you?

Can you explain how glass is made?

Can you explain how rocks are quarried?

What do trees have to do with the history of your area?

Why do you think non-native plants or plants that are moved on purpose or by accident to a new area can be harmful?

Are there disagreements going on right now where you live about how to use the land or water?

Alf Evers said there were always treasures in the mountains. What treasures do you think the mountains hold now?

Can you name three things people can do to help protect the Catskill Mountains?

If you were going to paint a picture of the scenery of the Catskills, what would you paint?

What are some fun places to visit in the Catskills?

Some people would argue that we should keep the mountains and the forests unspoiled and only allow hikers to use them. Others argue that anyone should be able to enjoy the beauty of the mountains or use them for any kind of recreation they want, including campers and vehicles. Who do you think has a better argument? Support your argument.

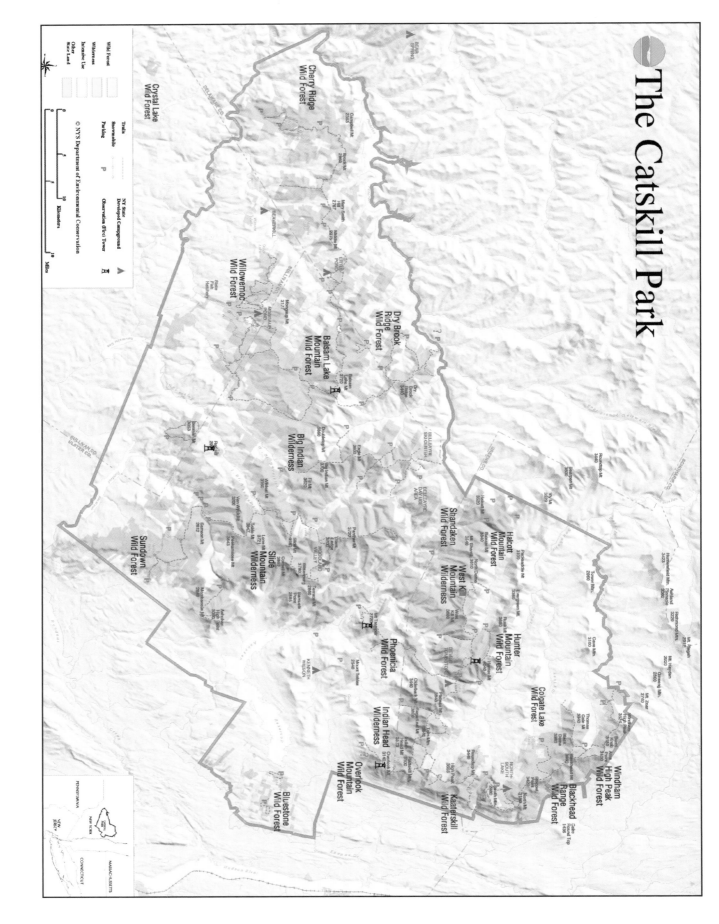

# The Catskill Park